I observe and watch and do
And, at times, I am thinking too!
Thoughts I could keep to myself
But better stored on high a shelf!

I came to this country from Holland in 1979 with my late husband and two sons. After a career in interior design and fashion, we started a small farm in Devon. I studied oil painting in Holland but switched to sculpture after my husband's death in 2001. My sculptures have featured regularly in local galleries and 'open studios'.

In 2017, I suddenly felt an urge to put my thoughts and every-day adventures into light hearted rhyme with simple illustrations. With the help and support of Jack, the dog, and the indespensable Rob (boots size 10), every Saturday and loads of optimism, I keep on enjoying it all.

Copyright © 2020 Michele Meyer
www.michelemeyer.net

Text and Illustrations by Michele Meyer
Cover Design by Michele Meyer
Formatted by Anna Ventura Artist & Designer

Printed by Kindle Direct Publishing

ISBN: 9798615292101

All rights reserved. No part of this book may be reproduced, stored or transmitted in any form, including within a retrieval system, without the prior written permission of the autor   .

CONTENTS
by page

4	Suspension	21	What a choice
5	Braces... continued	22	Ever decreasing circles
6	Continuity / March 2019	23	Guidelines and procedures
7	When it hits...	24	Birth of a baby boy
8	Waiting time	25	I weed and weed
9	The Power of the Sun	26	... more "Plantology"
10	A muddle and a puzzle 29/03/19	27	An anniversary
11	BIG LIES... or small lies	28	New skin, old skin
12	Passing into adulthood	29	Giraffe philosophy
13	An injured leg	30	Grandchildren
14	Jerusalem	31	The Dodo tale
15	History of transport	32	Cloud number 9
16	... more history of transport	33	12th of December (election day)
18	The radiologist	34	A smashing Boris win
19	A stranger's voice	35	HO HO HO ... X-mas time ... again
20	Leg or tail	36	New Year 2020

Suspension

With years you gain in confidence
And overall circumference.
You gain in wrinkles
Add some pimples.

Oh, there is a lot to gain!
But then you search in vain
For a waistline that is apt
To hold a belt and trousers up!

As you gain experience
The answer becomes evident.
Solution to my sinking trouser
I find swiftly on my Browser!
Braces in bright red
I order on the Net!

To find solutions is quite jolly
There is no need to lose your trolley.
Problem solved, battle won,
And my braces are such fun!

Braces... continued

My first outing with my braces
Wasn't to the Ascot races
But a sculpture exhibition
With some friends, an arty mission!

There was chit-chat, cups of tea
And suddenly I had to be
In the little lavatory

A big commotion in the loo
Will come as no surprise to you
Oh, you have to be so fit
To find that tiny little clip
Under garments worn on top
Oh... my braces are a flop!!

Unisex.... a good idea?
Not with braces, I do fear
When lowering my trousers fast...
I understand at last
That delightful little difference
Between the sexes is existing!

Continuity / March 2019

With knife crime, Brexit, women's week
There is a thing I really need
The feel of continuity
A place to give security.

I am so lucky to be old
Needn't do what I am told.
Never travel far afield
It's my village, that I need.

Post office, school, the local pub
Shop, village hall, the local hub.
Just to know it's all in place
Makes me happy, keeps me safe.

Kids are waiting for the bus
At nine o'clock there is a buzz.
Big guy with dog on lead
Attending to the doggie's needs.

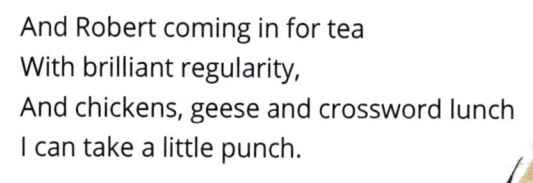

And Robert coming in for tea
With brilliant regularity,
And chickens, geese and crossword lunch
I can take a little punch.

When it hits

Occasionally the fan will hit
Bits of the proverbial shit!
Then it seems a good idea
To shut your eyes and not go near.

It's always good remembering
And try to be a kid again
Look at it with younger eyes
And ... surprise.... surprise.... surprise
It then will raise... a secret smile!

The kid in you will find it funny
(if the stuff is not too runny)
And will carry on in life
Taking things in easy stride.

Waiting time

I get new treatments for my ills
Thanks to the Doctor's learned skills.
There is a happy, grateful me
So eager, ready ..... plain to see!

All treatments come with info
Got to read them...... Doctor says so!
Listed are the side effects
And there we go... just lets!
I count them first, all forty-eight.
Ignoring them would tempt the fate.

I could turn yellow, cough a lot,
Feeling pain in certain spot,
Loosing hair, gaining weight,
Loosing sight, not seeing straight!
Or have the runs...and rather fast
There is more.... it's not the last!

On and on and on we go
They even show a video,
Offer thoughtful counselling
To check my mind.... the mood I'm in.

Is all that Info drowning me?
In an endless 'Info -Sea'?
The one thing that is saving me
Is a good old cup of milky tea!

The power of the sun

He is no King nor President
Just a kind of resident.
He has power and some fun
Giving Trump an easy run.

>Would we put Murdock to the test
Which interests would he serve the best?
He will tell us in black ink
How and what we all should think.
With Fox News, TV or daily paper
And two sons to follow later.

We needn't be afraid
His power will not fade!
There is no cream that will protect
From the Sun's prolonged effect.

Sailing around the open sea
I guess he watches with some glee
How we are sinking ever lower
While he is holding all that power.

A muddle and a puzzle 29/03/19

Gorgeous day, the sun is shining
Spring is here, I need reminding.
I got myself into a muddle
Try to solve it is a puzzle.

The English language is …. again
Taxing my old peasant brain.
It's more its use that puzzles me
It might just be a joke, you see!

At times officials warn with pride
If telling truth, and not just lie
The one times that their speech is clear
They will announce it, do not fear!
That makes clear language or the truth
Something they do seldom use!

I must say, that as a peasant,
I do not find that very pleasant
… but then, as humour figures highly
The reverse is also likely….
Announcing strongly to be true
They might just sell a lie to you.

Have I solved my little puzzle?
Or stepped into a deeper muddle?

Big lies... or small lies

When I was an eight-year-old
I tried to be real strong and bold,
And so it was a shameless lie
That got a smacking straight away!
As I still remember it
That punishment, it did the trick!

Nowadays they're warning you
Smack your kids and they will sue.
And in court you'd surely lose

And.... well ... to tell the truth:

If they are writing lies on buses
In great big letters tell the masses
How to vote with confidence
And never mind the consequence
You only find a judge, who would...
Let those bad boys off the hook
Have them vie for highest office.
And we look on thinking: 'sod it'.
If lies are pure political
They seem OK, acceptable!

As I am old, the odd white lie
I hesitatingly sometimes try
Bringing back the eight-year-old
Trying to be strong and bold!

Passing into adulthood

I sit and watch.... observe
How characters emerge
Teeners do excite me
With sudden changes likely!

.........the boy looked like a kiddy
To me, the ancient biddy.
He did a lot of lounging
In a corner crouching
With nothing but a fweel
For virtual reality.

But that was in the past
And now......at last...
I see a man in front of me
With such a great vitality.

He trimmed some trees
Removed the leaves
Returned the tool
An action new ...... sooo cool!
He said Goodbye to puberty
What a delight is that to see!

The sudden change, it happened
Is there a cheer and clapping?

An injured leg

The injured friend, she is on crutches
And she desperately clutches...
The biggest book as yet
More than a hundred pages fat!

She loves to lead a country life
The leg prevents the very strive.
Now she only turns the pages,
As, again, the season changes,
In pictures and in text
She waits what's coming next.
Seeing only text and picture
Life can be a boring fixture.
But clouds do have a silver lining
It needs looking and then finding!

Who brings you coffee, makes your tea?
You have a house-elf, don't you see?
Enjoy the little positives'
All will be better in a whiff
You grow your flowers once again
Looking for that elf in vain!
You wear again your garden glove!
I wish you strength and all my love.

THE HUSBAND

Jerusalem

(the WI's favourite hymn for all occasions Weddings, Funerals....the lot)

If only I could sing
And take away the sting
Of moving lips without a sound.
Just read the text…. it's so profound!
Then…think it through and read again
Try…. understand my fellow men.

United they sing loud and clear
Wishing Jerusalem were here.
Do they really wish for that?
Can't be true, I take a bet!

Crusaders gone there, sword in hand
Got there twice, drew lines in sand,
And you could say it left a mess.
For generations… and the rest.

But the congregation wows
To take their arrows and their bows
Even with a sword in hand
They would perpetuate that trend?

Surely, people on their own
Would hesitate and think and frown!
Not join in or not to sing
Is really quite embarrassing
I am… and I can tell
Not joining in ….is not so swell!

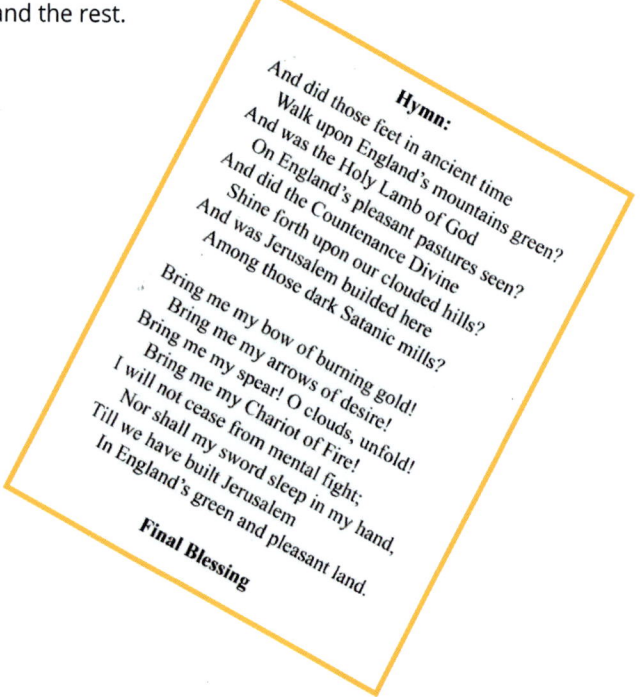

Hymn:

And did those feet in ancient time
Walk upon England's mountains green?
And was the Holy Lamb of God
On England's pleasant pastures seen?
And did the Countenance Divine
Shine forth upon our clouded hills?
And was Jerusalem builded here
Among those dark Satanic mills?

Bring me my bow of burning gold!
Bring me my arrows of desire!
Bring me my spear! O clouds, unfold!
Bring me my Chariot of Fire!
I will not cease from mental fight;
Nor shall my sword sleep in my hand,
Till we have built Jerusalem
In England's green and pleasant land.

Final Blessing

The history of transport

Transport has some history
The horse would trot from A to B
And carry you quiet far
Without a motor car.
Gladly pull your carriages
To drop you off at Claridge's.

They took their rider at a pace
From Inn to Inn, from place to place.
Or move the cannons out to war.
Their fate was cherished but quite raw.

Now the picture is reversed
They might still pull the royal hearse.
But normally WE drive them round
in a horsebox, safe and sound.
Assessing progress over years
Is a challenge, can be fierce!

The horse might have a great comeback
When climate change has more effect
And again make history
Trotting on from A to B......

... more history of transport

Inherent transport is indeed
Our sturdy legs and pair of feet.
We need them for commuting.
Then sit-down computing.
Safely behind office doors
Under desks on polished floors.
The feet control the gas
When moving round in cars.

Our legs could do much more
As did the ancient warrior!
They carried roman legions
To far flung Scottish regions
As proof they built a wall
In parts still standing tall

There always is a therapist
Keen to get you on the list
To join the local gym
To shape and tone and trim.
Where the treadmills stand in rows
Used by guys with sweaty brows
The legs, all moving, walk or run
Is it really that much fun?

An applause for effort seems in order
But will they ever reach the Scottish border?

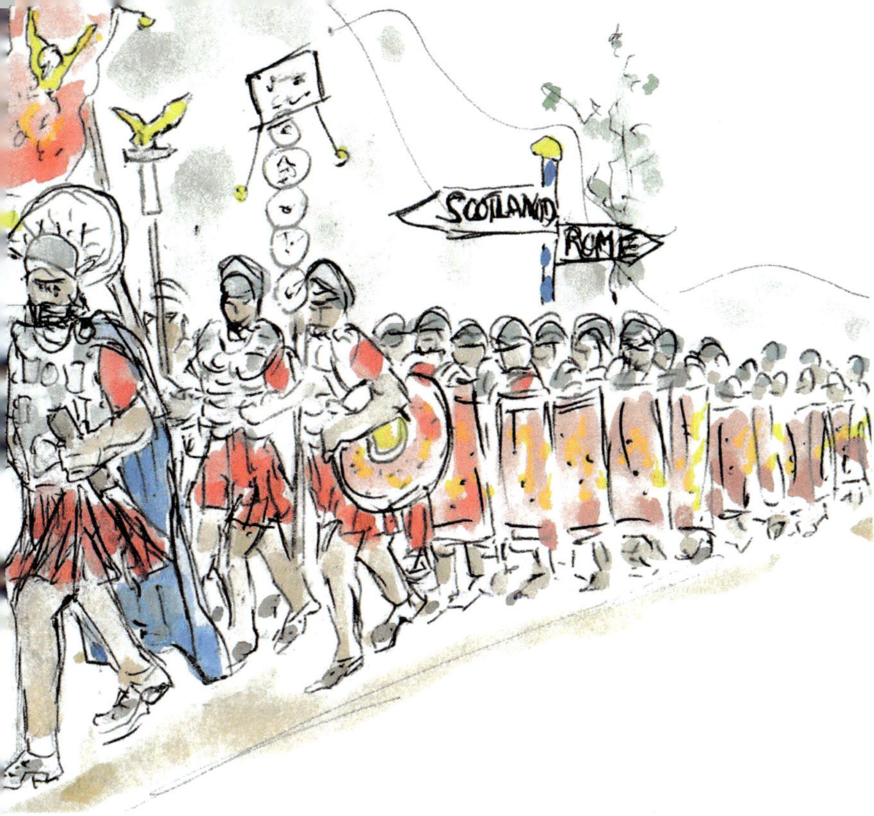
SCOTLAND
ROME

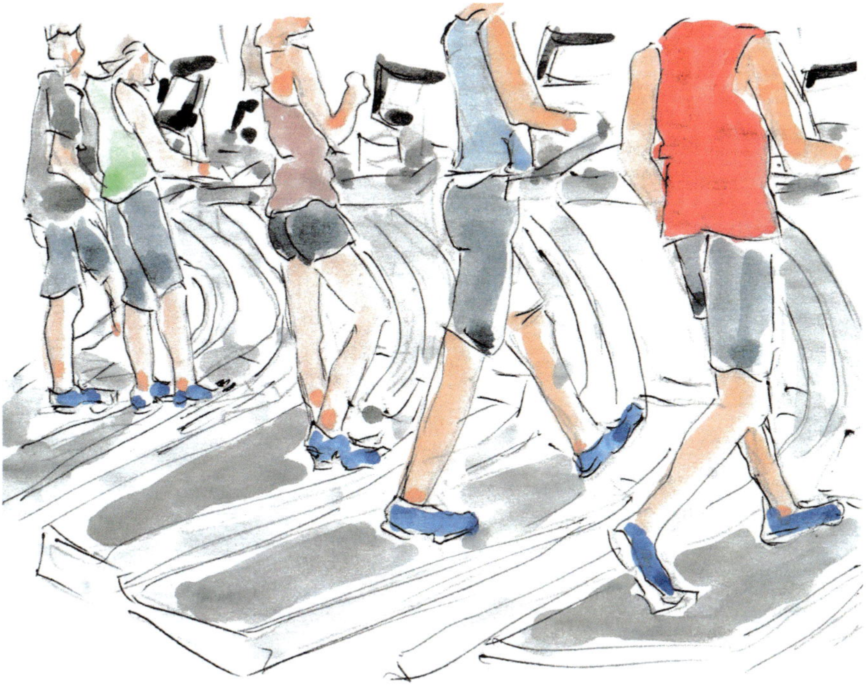

The radiologist

My inners are an open book
To you, as you intensely look
From slide to slide
From side to side
And with another cup of tea
You analyse the stuff you see.
There are reactions to the tracer
To be compared a little later.

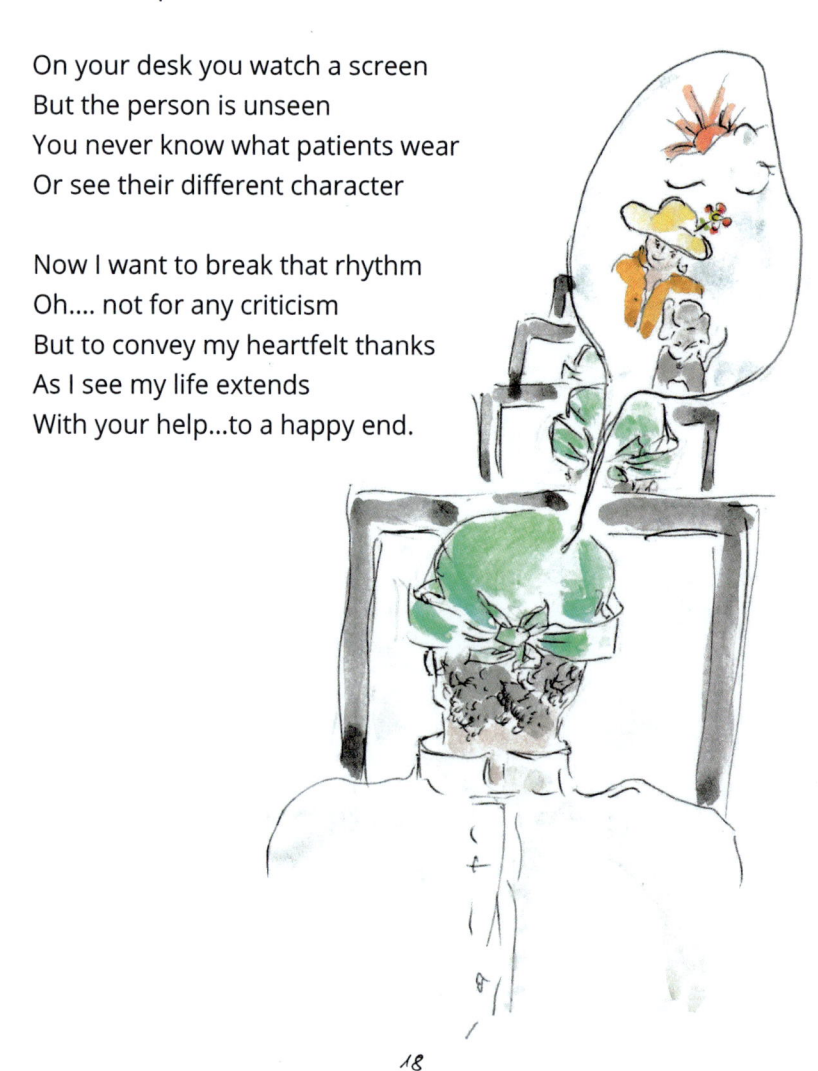

On your desk you watch a screen
But the person is unseen
You never know what patients wear
Or see their different character

Now I want to break that rhythm
Oh…. not for any criticism
But to convey my heartfelt thanks
As I see my life extends
With your help…to a happy end.

A stranger's voice

Pick up the phone, is there a choice?
...and I hear a stranger's voice:
'I stayed with you, Michele my dear
2012 that was the year.
It was so lovely then
So, could we meet again?

You MUST remember, yes you do!'
...But do I have the slightest clue?
Can I tell him hand on heart?
His visit left no single mark
On my ageing memory
It could be John or Marc or Ian
I might know him when I see him!

But to declare this dire fact
Is not the answer.... with respect!

So, faking enthusiastically
A great welcome.... friendly feel
I invite him actually
To come and share a meal with me.

And what an evening we had
Sharing wine, a hearty snack
Faking might just in the end
Deliver home a long-lost friend.

Leg or tail

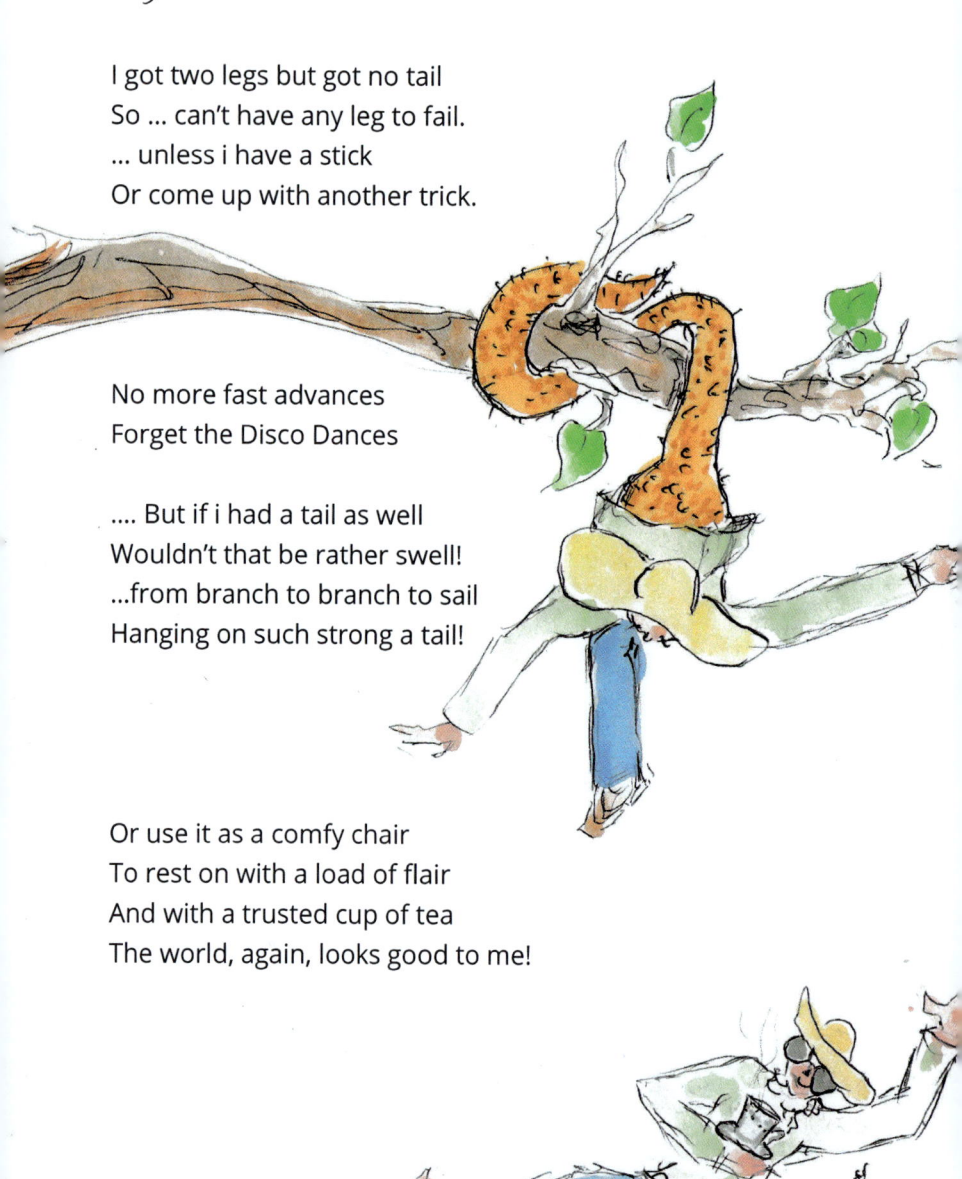

I got two legs but got no tail
So ... can't have any leg to fail.
... unless i have a stick
Or come up with another trick.

No more fast advances
Forget the Disco Dances

.... But if i had a tail as well
Wouldn't that be rather swell!
...from branch to branch to sail
Hanging on such strong a tail!

Or use it as a comfy chair
To rest on with a load of flair
And with a trusted cup of tea
The world, again, looks good to me!

What a choice

Getting married, all that stuff
…… when I am forty, soon enough!
My teenage dream was clear
No marriage yet, no fear.
A thing I had preferred by far
Was an E-type Jaguar!

Bright Ideas I had a plenty
Then got married at age just twenty.
He had a lovely Labrador
With loads of puppies, I adore!

They helped in making the decision
To forget my previous vision.
Now I am widowed with a dog
It's Jack, he eats a lot.
… yes, you guessed it, say no more
It had to be a Labrador!

Ever decreasing circles

As Great Britain moves around
In decreasing circles ...inward bound
My verses lose their lightness,
Joy, happiness and brightness.

I am putting into rhyme
Reflections of our time.

Carelessness and showmanship
Care for Country.... not a bit!
Leaders being power chancers
Moving round like Morris Dancers.

Circles I see everywhere
I treat my own with greatest care.
It's limiting and getting smaller
Surrounded by a scented border
With Honeysuckle, Jasmin, Thyme
For the moment we are fine.

Guidelines and procedures

Guidelines and procedures
What will they ever cure?
Who knows who writes the stuff?
It's never ever one of us!
Efficiency should cure our ills
Regardless of a doctor's skills

Politics, Economy
Guidelines rule so cunningly.
Directives set, come what will,
Waiting times extending still!
Doctors know the consequence
Are they asked for reference?

To survive you need some wit
Be really strong and fighting fit!

I gather strength on garden chair
My darling geese are also there
And we enjoy our little moan,
With them and Jack I am not alone!

With the ever-saving cup of tea
There is nothing that can worry me!

Birth of a little boy

After rolling in the tummy
Of your ever loving mummy
It's time to face the world, my boy
Bringing purpose, love and joy!

And there you are so sweet and cute
In your pinkish birthday suit.
They dress you up with woollen sock
To help you face the sudden shock.

From darkness to a light so bright
Do try to face it with delight!
You will be very tall and strong…
And clever too…. don't get me wrong!

You made a clever choice of parent
With so much love and care apparent!
A heart felt welcome my dear boy
We wish you happiness and joy!

→ woolen sock

I weed & weed

I weed and weed…. and it grows back
No change in overall effect!
Take chick weed or azalea
Dandelion and dahlia
All green and growing living plants
Do they enjoy same fate or chance?
Rules start at the garden gate
There we decide and allocate.

We know two types of plants:
Weeds put on a common stance
But the elite you get in pots
And they do cost a lot.

Being Dutch, I am quite mean
Spending money…. not so keen!
Let it grow, let it be
And soon enough you might well see
My garden in the 'jungle- look'
Oh, it does look rather good!
In between my giant plants
The nettle even stands a chance!
And if you ever look for me
Deep in the jungle I will be

With a healthy cup of nettle tea

... more "Plantology"

I am feeling like a garden gnome
Do lots of thinking on my own.
Another sample coming here
Might not be that crystal clear:

I think there is a hierarchy
In the plant society!
Under glass the 'posh 'ones grow
Lined up in a perfect row.
Far from nature they grow up
Not like the common Buttercup.
Privilege and good manure
They gobble up with some allure.

Weeds work on the other hand
With endurance and intend
To occupy the empty spaces
To swiftly be eradicated.
The classy ones will need the room
To grow and ...maybe bloom.

Will I honour the persistence and endeavour
Shown so bravely and for ever
By Dandelion and Buttercup?
And just enjoy the 'giving up'?

An anniversary

What is behind the flushing bride
Or the groom's attractive stride?
It's a secret so exciting
You remember the first sighting?

Entering year twenty-five
You continue in your strive
To make every minute count
In the company you found!

A lifetime of discovery
In love respect and harmony.
Enjoy the journey step by step
And happiness falls in your lap.

New skin... old skin

Unbeknown to most of us
And without the slightest fuss
Monthly our skin renews
The old flakes are of little use.
It happens to us unaware
We do not in the slightest care.

Thinking of the snake instead
She sheds her skin complete.... intact.
Just simply sliding out of it
And there it is ... for us to pick.

To shed our skin in one event
Should become a novel trend
Leaving the old skin behind
Newly clad we then will find
That it's undeniable:
Old skin is compostable.

Giraffe philosophy

Oh why, oh why it isn't me?

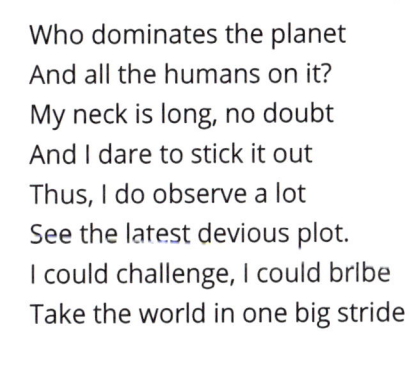

Who dominates the planet
And all the humans on it?
My neck is long, no doubt
And I dare to stick it out
Thus, I do observe a lot
See the latest devious plot.
I could challenge, I could bribe
Take the world in one big stride

..... but rather do Philosophy
Much less effort, don't you see?
Think in my hammock I will do
... Can surely leave the rest to you!

Grandkids

Grandkids can be rather cute
But I prefer the older brood
The age they tell me when I'm wrong
And check my fridge and goings on!

But now that both are studying
I wonder where my genes come in.
Then suddenly, my eyebrows rise
And to my great surprise
They ask me for survival skills
Not just the common headache pills.
I thought they didn't give a s......
For any smelly rural bit.

How to skin a rabbit fast...
A skill that would for ever last.
Two bunnies came, they were not asked,
But lay ready for the task
Skinning rabbits
Was a habit
Back in the deepest past
And didn't last.

But there you go, you never know
You might not find a ready cow!
But will be safe and well
Just catch a rabbit in the dell!

The Dodo tale (or the failed replica)

The Dodo is so very dead
I'm sure we never ever met.
And on reflection ….
There is no interaction.
If i have a closer look
He should be in a Disney book!

You want a replica in clay
I tried… but have to say
My skills are just not good enough
To my regret… I am giving up!

Will fiction ever be
The new reality?
Could we adapt and change
Into a robotic range?
Where would life and nature be?
What a thought, oh dearie me!

There are real birds, far less dead
Overlooked or never met!
And surely. from my side
I enjoy them with delight.
And so I fill the feeder….
On peanuts they are eager!

Cloud number 9

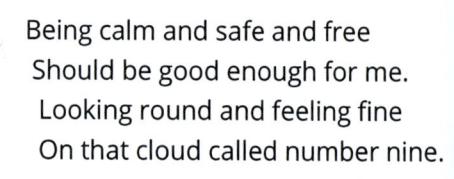

Being calm and safe and free
Should be good enough for me.
Looking round and feeling fine
On that cloud called number nine.

But come November dark and cold
It's less comfy on my cloud!
I climb down the many steps
To escape the worst effects.

No more going high and higher
Better light a warming fire.
Is it just the time of year?
Or is it other stuff, I fear?
Have I become that wobbly,
Or the globe supporting me?

But in the end, predictably
I pour myself a cup of tea!
Take the wobble of the menu
And make my home a happy venue.

12th of December (election day)

Opinions matter
So you better...
Draw a cross and make your choice!
But do we really have a voice?

That choice is almost binary
With no convincing plan to see
Should we straight away dismiss
All those lies and promises
It's Labour or the Eton crowd,
They have to really fight it out!

Ending in a boxing game
All excitement all the same!
Book yourself a ringside seat
And watch the boxing match proceed!

I am lucky ......cannot vote
But I know what it's about.
So, I send my X-mas cards
With a stamp real second class!

A smashing Boris win (13/12/19)

In the ring he fought it out
Bulging muscle without doubt
Drove a truck through fake brick wall
That's what did it after all!
He is the winner, standing tall
To smash whatever...great or small!
Walls to jump, walls to scale
And he doesn't like to fail!
His style seemed so appealing
But now it comes to dealing
With all the promises he made
Rather sooner, not too late!
After all it's about power
Loosing that would make him sour!

And I could think of something cooler
......than a great big sulking ruler!

HO HO HO... Xmas time... again

We are meant to tow the line
At this special X-mas time,
Being normal after all
Isn't normal any more!
Out come the X-mas jumpers
And fake old reindeer antlers!

When getting nearer to December
I weaken and surrender
To all the glitter and the hype
Got to take it in my stride!
To avoid it would be risky
Better join in and be frisky!
After all, in candle light,
The world seems warm and light and bright!

New Year 2020

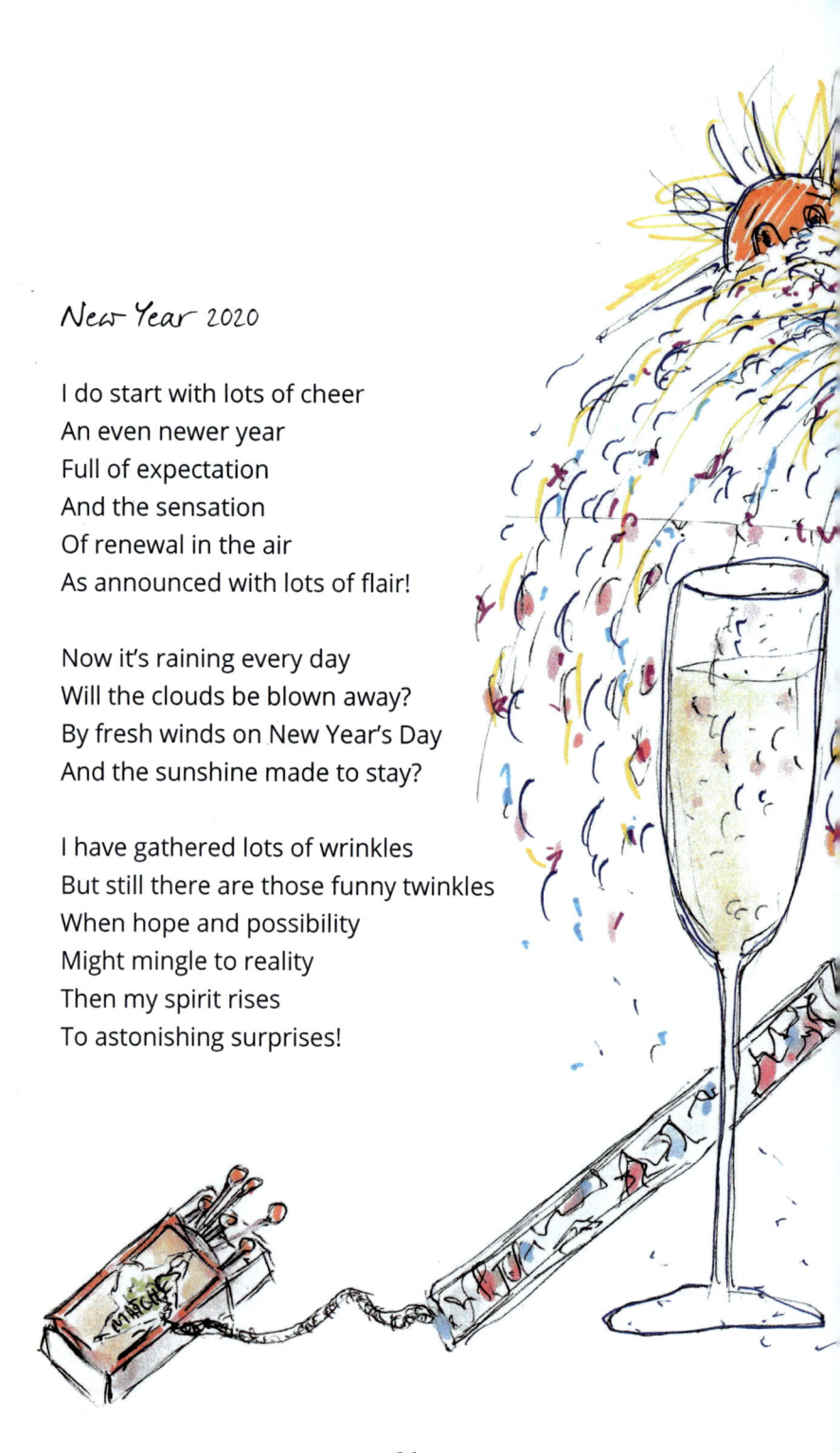

I do start with lots of cheer
An even newer year
Full of expectation
And the sensation
Of renewal in the air
As announced with lots of flair!

Now it's raining every day
Will the clouds be blown away?
By fresh winds on New Year's Day
And the sunshine made to stay?

I have gathered lots of wrinkles
But still there are those funny twinkles
When hope and possibility
Might mingle to reality
Then my spirit rises
To astonishing surprises!